To Nikita & Isha —

Dream Big!?
Live Bigger!

For Adela, Elaina, Faith and Zannah Rose. - MB

For Julia Matott who dreamed big and taught me to.
To Andy, you have made many of my dreams come true. - JM

For Lauren, who I love and believe in...
completely. - ML

Text Copyright © 2005 Skoob Books
Illustration Copyright © 2005 Mark Ludy

Printed by Everbest Printing Co., Nansha, China
Production Date: June 2010

Batch #: 1

Third Printing
2010

SKOOB BOOKS
PO Box 631183
Littleton, CO 80163
www.justinmatott.com

Baker, Margaret.
Ludy, Mark.
Matott, Justin.
When I Was A Girl... I Dreamed /
Written by Justin Matott & Margaret Baker /
Illustrations by Mark Ludy.
3rd Ed.
p. cm.

Library of Congress Control Number: 2005925139
ISBN 1-889191-25-6

WHEN I WAS A GIRL I DREAMED

WRITTEN BY

MARGARET BAKER & JUSTIN MATOTT

ILLUSTRATED BY

MARK LUDY

SKOOBBOOKS
publishing house
colorado

When I was a girl, I dreamed great dreams

of who I'd be and where,

of places near and journeys far,

adventures wild and rare.

I dreamed I was the teacher,

of an eager, lively class.

I taught them reading, writing, math,

and prayed they all would pass.

Many of my students

led extraordinary lives.

Imagine my joy when one naughty boy

received the Nobel Prize!

I dreamed I was a dancer,

so graceful, so refined.

Directors longed to sign me on,

and roles for me designed.

I jumped and twirled up on my toes.

I leapt and soared so high.

A princess in my pale pink shoes,

I felt like I could fly.

I dreamed I was an artist,

studied brushstrokes, mastered hues,

and painted on my canvas

the world's most splendid views.

My landscapes were in great demand.

The art world knew my name.

What a delight to know my work

had earned such lasting fame.

I dreamed I cared for animals,

for every kind of beast,

from the strong and mighty rhino

to the smallest and the least.

My patients came from far and wide,

from every stripe and nation.

I even cured the jungle king!

(I had quite a reputation).

I dreamed I built a robot

who could vacuum, cook and clean.

She even washed my windows!

What a marvelous machine.

She'd paint my nails and comb my hair,

then fix my supper, fast.

A fantastic friend, my robot maid,

we really had a blast!

I dreamed I was a diver

who explored the seas down deep.

I studied coral reefs and sea life

and exotic things that creep.

Such an awesome mass of fish,

each one with its own style.

What a joy to take close-ups

and to see that great white smile.

I dreamed I floated 'round the world

in a huge hot air balloon.

From L.A. to New York

on a sunny afternoon.

I saw mountains, valleys, cities, towns,

and oceans shore to shore.

All Seven Wonders of the World,

then discovered several more.

I dreamed I lived in Egypt,

seeking artifacts so rare.

I burrowed under pyramids

to see what might be there.

And what I found, you won't believe,

deep beneath the earth,

The Tomb of the Five Kings!

Of immense and untold worth.

I dreamed I had a clubhouse

that was stationed up in space.

I invited all my friends to come

to that exciting place.

We'd play volleyball and checkers,

talk at poolside, share a snack.

Though it was far, my rocket car

would zoom us there and back.

I dreamed I rode my faithful horse

out in the wild Wild West.

I rounded up the bandits,

and proved I was the best!

I hauled those villains into town

and restored the rule of law.

Was presented with the city's key.

The mayor was in awe.

I dreamed I was an athlete,

playing basketball for "State."

That season we won every game.

Our teamwork was first-rate.

We made it to the finals,

all tied, the clock near zero.

I jumped, I aimed, I shot,

I SCORED! That night I was the hero.

I dreamed I owned a shopping mall,

and went on quite a spree.

I bought odds and ends for all my friends,

and even some for me.

Shoes and purses, jewelry, hats,

in boxes stacked so tall.

With a pair of dapper butlers

at our every beck and call.

I dreamed I was the President,

the leader of my land.

My goal was not to rule,

but rather seek to understand.

And so I listened closely,

read each postcard, every letter.

And together with all citizens,

we made our country better.

I dreamed that I wrote stories

of princesses and lords.

I even won a Newbery

and other book awards.

But the notes my readers sent to me

gave me far more pleasure.

To know that I'd inspired their hearts,

that is my greatest treasure.

Yes, as a girl I dreamed great dreams.

Perhaps you dream them too.

Reach higher than the stars, my dears,

and your dreams...

will come true.